Santa Claus:
SUPER SPY

The Case of the
Minnesota Minotaur

by Ryan Jacobson

Illustrated by Monica Bruenjes

Emelyn, Grayson,
+ Oliver,
Stay super!

Mora, Minnesota

*For John Kvamme and Paul Scholten,
childhood friends who fostered my imagination.*

Special thanks to Becky and Noah; to Eddie, Gracie and Heidi Johnson; and to Cheri Jacobson.

Based on character designs by Erica Belkholm
Cover art and page 5 art by Katy Farina
Interior art by Monica Bruenjes

Author photo by Laura Parson, from Laura Linnea Photography
Santa Claus: Super Spy logo by Ryan Jacobson

10 9 8 7 6 5 4 3 2 1

ISBN: 978-0-9881842-1-3

Super Spy
Secret Code

1 = A	10 = J	19 = S
2 = B	11 = K	20 = T
3= C	12 = L	21 = U
4 = D	13 = M	22 = V
5 = E	14 = N	23 = W
6 = F	15 = O	24 = X
7 = G	16 = P	25 = Y
8 = H	17 = Q	26 = Z
9 = I	18 = R	

Can you solve this secret message from Santa Claus?

The first letter is filled in for you.

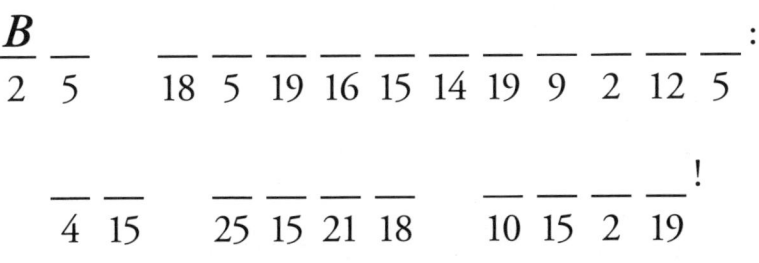

B __   __ __ __ __ __ __ __ __ __ __ __ :
2 5   18 5 19 16 15 14 19 9 2 12 5

__ __   __ __ __ __   __ __ __ __ !
4 15   25 15 21 18   10 15 2 19

Contents

What Is a Super Spy?

Santa has a secret. He's a Super Spy. With the help of boys and girls across the country, he protects the world from danger.

Now, Santa and his top agents, Paul Jenkins and Emily Swanson, will use their Super Spy watches and gadget belts. They must save the state of Minnesota from a giant monster . . .

1
A New Pet

"I promise to take care of it," Paul Jenkins said.

The boy had been asking for a puppy since last Christmas. Each time, he made that same promise.

"Playing with a puppy is fun," said Paul's dad. "But what about when it makes a mess? Will you clean it up?"

Paul nodded. "I will. And I'll feed it. I'll take it for walks. I will do everything!"

"I can help, too," added Paul's brother.

Matt was only five years old. So Paul knew he could not help as much.

Mr. Jenkins smiled. "Okay, boys. Your mom and I agree. Let's get a dog."

Paul jumped in the air and cheered.

* * * * *

The puppy was smaller than a teddy bear. It had a skinny body and short, brown fur. It looked like a tiny reindeer. So Paul named it Rainy.

Rainy liked to run and jump. Paul liked to chase Rainy. Matt did, too, for a while. But Matt got bored of that game. Paul never did.

Paul was there when Rainy made a mess on the carpet. The smell was awful! Paul acted like he didn't see the brown goo. He hoped someone else would clean it. No one did.

Paul tried to get close to the mess. It made him gag. He almost barfed.

I can't clean Rainy's mess, Paul thought. *No way! But I know who will.*

"Matt," Paul whispered. "You promised to help me take care of Rainy."

Matt smiled and nodded.

"Your job is to clean up the poo," said Paul.

Matt's smile became a frown. "Do I have to?"

"You promised," Paul replied.

Matt looked down and shook his head. But he did as he was told.

It took Matt a long time. He scrubbed and scrubbed. He ended up with brown on his arms and shirt. That made him cry.

Paul knew that he should help Matt. But the smell was too stinky. So Paul just watched. He felt like crying, too.

2
Messy Campers

Minnesota was famous for its cold winters. But the summers got pretty hot. This summer night was a warm one.

Bob and Amy were with four of their friends. They were in a northern part of the state. The area was called the Boundary Waters.

Minnesota was the Land of 10,000 Lakes. Its capital was the city of Saint Paul.

The Mall of America was the state's most busy place. But Minnesota was best known for its fishing and camping.

That was why Bob and Amy were in the Boundary Waters. It was full of forests and lakes. It was a perfect place for fishing and camping.

Most people helped to keep the Boundary Waters clean. Most, but not all.

"We need more wood for the fire," said Bob.

"Break branches off a tree," Amy answered. "It's bad for the tree. But I want to roast marshmallows."

Bob tossed his garbage to the side. He watched it float away in the wind. Then he jogged to a small tree. He broke off a stack of thin branches.

Bob carried the wood back to the fire. Then he dropped it in. The flame grew big and bright. Bob felt heat on his skin.

Boom!

The sound came from deep in the forest.

"What was that?" asked Amy. Her voice shook when she spoke.

Bob laughed. "It must be Paul Bunyan. He's a giant. The sound was his giant step."

His friends laughed, too.

"Paul Bunyan isn't real," said Amy.

"He's just a tall tale," Bob agreed. "He isn't real, but there are lots of legends about him. His pet was a big blue ox named Babe. One story says that the lakes in Minnesota are their footprints."

Everyone laughed again, even Amy.

"A giant with a blue ox?" she said. "That's crazy."

Boom!

The noise came back. It was louder this time.

Boom!

There it was again. It almost sounded as if . . .

Boom!

. . . it was getting closer . . .

Boom!

. . . and closer . . .

A huge shape appeared at the edge of the campsite. The shape was so tall that it blocked the moon.

Boom!

The campers heard the sound once more. This time, a giant foot crashed between them. It squashed their fire.

Bob looked up. He saw the very large legs of a man. He saw the very large body of a man. But he did not see the very large head of a man. That would have been scary. He saw something much worse.

Bob screamed. His friends did, too.

And then they ran for their lives.

3
Mission: Minnesota

The buzzing noise scared Paul. He opened his eyes, but he could not see. His bedroom was still dark. The moon shined through his window.

The buzzing noise came again. Paul's Super Spy watch glowed.

"It must be a message from Santa Claus," Paul said to himself. "A call in the middle of the night? This could be important."

He grabbed his watch and looked at the screen. He saw a series of numbers. It was a message sent in the Super Spy secret code.

2-5-8-9-14-4
20-8-5
7-1-18-1-7-5

A is one. B is two. C is three. And so on, thought Paul. *That means the first word is B-E-H-I-N-D.*

He solved the rest of the code. Then he read it out loud. "Behind the garage? Oh, Santa must be waiting for me."

Paul got dressed, and he raced outside. He found Santa's sleigh behind the garage. Santa Claus was standing beside it.

"Ho! Ho! Ho!" Santa laughed. "It's good to see you, Paul."

Most people thought Santa had magic powers. But that wasn't quite true. He was a great inventor. Most of his powers came from his crazy inventions. Paul and his friend Emily used some inventions on their Super Spy missions. They wore gadget belts with many different gadgets inside. Some of Paul's favorites were the Shoe Fly, the You-You, and the Trouble Bubble bubble gum.

"You look older, Paul," Ervin the Elf sang. "My, you've gotten tall."

Paul smiled at Ervin's rhyme. "I'm glad you came. Do we have a mission?"

"Yes, we do," Santa replied. "Let's go and get Emily. Then I'll tell you about it."

* * * * *

Emily was outside when the sleigh landed. She hopped in and hugged Paul. The sleigh shot into the air. The Super Spies were on their way to Minnesota.

There was only one reindeer leading the sleigh: Comet. Paul always felt amazed to see the reindeer

flying. He asked, "How do your reindeer fly, Santa? Most reindeer can't."

Santa grinned. "Their flying powers come from a machine I built. It's called the Power Switch. I use it to switch animal powers from one critter to the next. Can you guess what I mix with reindeer to make them fly?"

"I know," said Emily. "Birds."

"Ho! Ho! Ho!" Santa boomed. "That's right. But not just any birds. I mix them with Peregrine Falcons. They're the fastest birds in the world."

"Does your machine hurt the birds?" Paul asked.

"Of course, not," Santa answered. "But there was an accident once. A glowing bug, called a firefly, got mixed in with the reindeer and the bird. That reindeer got the power to fly—and a glowing nose."

Paul and Emily looked at each other. They nodded their heads and laughed.

Santa giggled, too. "Yes, that was funny. But the Power Switch could be dangerous. I must always be careful with it."

The sun began to rise. Comet led the sleigh toward the ground. Paul looked out and gasped. The sky was a blend of pink, purple, and gold. The lakes looked like mirrors of the sky. Large, green trees covered the rest of the land.

It was one of the most beautiful places Paul had ever seen. The Super Spies were at the Boundary Waters of Minnesota.

4

Camping Out

Santa landed the sleigh at the edge of a vast forest. He guided the sleigh into a thick group of trees. Then the team of Super Spies hopped out.

"We need a place to camp," said Santa. "That will be our base for this mission." He looked at Ervin and Comet. "Stay with the sleigh. We'll let you know if we need help."

"We will wait here. Do not fear," Ervin replied.

The jolly old man led Paul and Emily away. They hiked toward a large lake. It took a very long time to reach it.

When they got there, Paul was wet with sweat. His legs were sore, too. But he liked the Boundary Waters. The place was calm and quiet. Everything was green, and there were no buildings.

The lake stretched out as far as Paul could see. But it wasn't just water in front of him. The lake was dotted with islands, large ones and small ones.

Santa Claus pointed to an island in the distance. "Do you see that one, way out there?" he asked.

The children nodded.

"That's halfway across the lake. We'll rest when we get there. Then we'll cross the other half of the lake and set up camp."

Emily said, "Oh, no, I can't swim that far."

"Ho! Ho! Ho!" Santa laughed. "That would be a long way to swim. But I have a gadget that can help us. It's called a Can New." He pulled a tiny can out of his gadget belt. It shined like it was new.

"How can that help?" asked Paul.

Santa pulled off the lid. A small, flat piece of plastic popped out. It started filling up with air. It got bigger and began to look like a boat.

"A Can New," Santa said again. "It's a can with a canoe in it."

Paul and Emily found Can News in their gadget belts, too.

A few minutes later, the three Super Spies sat in their canoes and paddled atop the lake.

* * * * *

The trio ate lunch at the island. Then they paddled to the other side of the lake. There, they set up tents and started a campfire.

To Paul, it felt like the hottest day of summer. The fire was for cooking dinner.

Paul's shoulders hurt. His arms felt wobbly, like warm noodles. This had been a hard day. And he loved it. But he had been sweating for hours. He wished he could cool off.

"I know you're tired," Santa said. "But we're not done yet. Two of us should look for clues. One of us must stay and watch the fire. If we don't, the fire could get out of control. That might start the whole forest on fire."

Paul raised his hand. "I'll stay and watch it. I'm not afraid to be alone. And I'm very responsible."

Santa nodded. "Yes, I believe you are. Emily will come with me. We'll be back soon."

Santa and Emily hurried into the forest. Paul sat next to the fire. He watched it, and he waited.

5
Danger in the Woods

Paul was still sweating. He checked his watch. It had been 20 minutes since Santa and Emily left. He moved to the shade of a nearby tree. He tried to fan himself with his hands. It didn't help. He could not escape the heat.

He looked at the campfire again. The flames were almost gone. The wood had become a pile of white ashes.

A swim in the lake would feel good, Paul thought. *It could be quick: just a minute or two. Plus, the fire is nearly out. There's not much danger.*

Paul looked at the campfire once more. He nodded and said, "I'll be right back." Then he ran to the lake.

* * * * *

"What's this case about?" Emily asked. "Why are we here?"

Santa shrugged. "I don't know a lot, yet. All I can say is some campers saw a monster."

"What kind of monster?" replied Emily.

"Do you know what a minotaur is?" asked the jolly old man.

"I think so," Emily said. "Isn't it from an old myth? In the story, it had the body of a man and the head of a bull."

Santa smiled. "That's right. The campers saw a minotaur. We need to see if they're telling the truth."

Emily stopped walking. She stared down and said, "I think they were telling the truth."

She pointed at the ground in front of her. There was a huge footprint, the size of a car.

Santa gasped. "Oh, my, that's one big boot. Good job, Emily. You found a clue."

The two Super Spies walked in the direction of the footprint. They found another print. And then another. And then another.

They heard a sound from far away. It was as if someone was sawing wood. Or maybe driving a loud boat.

They hiked toward the sound. It got clearer, and Emily recognized it. The sound was like the noise her dad made when he slept. It was snoring. But it was much louder.

"The minotaur must be sleeping," she said.

Santa agreed. "This is our chance to catch it."

The snoring began to mix with a new sound. It was like a crowd cheering at a football game. That noise came from behind them.

The Super Spies looked back. A cloud of black smoke rose into the air.

Santa Claus exclaimed, "That's too much smoke. It's coming from our campsite!"

* * * * *

The first thing Paul noticed was the odor. The entire forest smelled like roasting marshmallows. It made him feel hungry.

Next, he heard the roar. It was like an airplane flying above his head. A blast of heat dried his body. It also caused him to sweat again.

Paul realized that the forest around him looked hazy. A black fog seemed to cover the land.

A bright light began to shine. It cut through the fog and hurt Paul's eyes. For a second, Paul had a crazy idea. He thought the sun had crashed into Minnesota.

And then he remembered. *The campfire,* he thought. *It started the forest on fire.*

6
Fire Fighters

Paul's eyes burned from the smoke. His shorts felt dry from the heat. He put on his T-shirt, socks, and shoes. Then he snapped his gadget belt around his waist. *I have to put out that fire,* he thought. *This is my fault.*

He reached into his gadget belt. He pulled out two wing-like stickers. *These Shoe Flies will allow me to fly,* he thought. *That way, I can see how big the fire is.*

Paul slapped the stickers onto his shoes. Tiny wings popped out and lifted him into the air. He soared high above the fire and dodged the clouds of smoke. When he looked down, he almost cried out.

The fire wasn't just at the campsite. It wasn't just on a nearby tree. The fire seemed to be everywhere. It filled an area larger than a school playground. And as Paul felt wind blow against him, he watched the fire grow.

"What am I going to do?" he said to himself.

Santa and Emily soon joined him in the sky. Both of them wore their Shoe Flies, too. Santa looked more angry than Paul had ever seen him before. Paul thought the not-so-jolly old man would yell at him.

Instead, Santa said, "Both of you, spread out. Fly above opposite ends of the fire. Then start chewing your Trouble Bubble bubble gum."

That was another gadget in their belts. It let each of them blow a giant bubble. When the bubble

burst, it made a gummy, sticky mess. (Emily had once used the gum to catch a villain.) It also sent special fireworks into the sky—a signal for help.

"How will that help us?" Emily asked. "The fire department won't get here in time."

Santa shook his head. "We're not calling for help. There isn't time. Both of you must blow the biggest bubbles you can. When the bubbles pop, the gum will fall onto the fire. There might be enough gum to cover the fire and put it out."

Paul flew to the edge of the fire and threw the gum into his mouth. He chewed it as fast as he could. Then he started to blow.

For a moment, he could see Emily across from him. She was doing the same. Then a big, pink bubble blocked his view. The bubble became bigger than him. Bigger than a car. Bigger than a house.

At last, he heard a popping noise. It sounded like thunder. It was followed by another *pop*. The Trouble Bubbles had burst. Thick blankets of gum fell onto the fire. Fireworks blasted into the sky, but the smoke hid them.

Some of the smoke cleared away, and Paul looked down at the fire. It was much smaller—only the size of his backyard.

But it still wasn't out.

7

A Giant Problem

Paul flew down to Santa. Emily arrived at the same time. But Paul could barely see her. Thick smoke still filled the air.

"What are we going to do?" Paul shouted over the fire's roar.

Santa Claus shook his head. He began to say, "I don't—." His voice was cut off by a loud *whoosh*!

Paul felt something hit the top of his head. It rolled down his body. It felt cold—and good. He realized that he was all wet. Santa and Emily were, too.

The smoke grew even thicker. It hissed. The fire sounded more like a snake than a roaring crowd. And it didn't feel quite as hot.

Paul did not understand. What happened to the fire? Where did the water come from? How did he get so wet?

Santa seemed to know. "The fire's out," he said. "Someone dumped water on it."

"How can that be?" asked Emily. "The fire was so big. It would take a lot of water . . ."

She didn't finish her sentence. She didn't need to. The smoke began to clear, and the Super Spies saw the answer to their questions.

The giant minotaur was standing next to them. It must have poured lake water onto the fire.

Now that the flames were out, the heroes had another job to do.

"Catch that minotaur!" Santa shouted.

Paul and Emily soared into the sky. The beast growled in anger. It tried to swat them with its large hands. The children buzzed around it like bees.

Paul could not think of a gadget to use against the giant. And his Shoe Flies were running out of energy. He would have to land soon. Paul hoped that Santa had a plan.

The minotaur stomped its foot. Paul saw Santa roll out of the way. Santa reached into his belt. He pulled out a small gadget. It was one Paul had seen before.

The item looked like a freeze ray, but that wasn't what it was. It was called a Shrink Wrapper. Santa normally used it to shrink and wrap presents. (That way, the presents all fit in his sleigh.) Santa had also once used it to shrink a dinosaur.

Paul guessed Santa's plan. The jolly old man was going to shrink this monster down to their size.

The minotaur stomped again and again. Santa kept dodging the huge boots. But he didn't see the minotaur's giant hand swinging toward him.

The hand swatted Santa. He flew past several trees before landing with a *thud*. He also dropped the Shrink Wrapper. It bounced away from him.

Paul watched in horror. The minotaur's giant foot came down hard. The foot missed Santa. But it smashed the Shrink Wrapper to pieces.

8
A New Plan

There was no time to lose. Santa was about to be squashed by the minotaur. Paul looked at Emily and nodded. Then the two Super Spies sped toward their boss.

As they darted past him, each child grabbed one of his arms. They flew him away from danger, just as the minotaur stomped its foot again.

Santa groaned. He was still hurt from hitting the ground. He was in no shape to battle a monster. Plus, the Super Spies needed a new plan. They flew far away from the minotaur.

When the Shoe Flies ran out of energy, the trio landed. Paul looked back. He was glad that the monster was not chasing them.

For now, the heroes were safe. And they needed to rest. Paul helped Santa lie down. Then he sat next to him. He leaned against a tree and closed his eyes. Paul fell asleep before he could count to ten.

* * * * *

Paul opened his eyes. He saw Santa staring at him. The old man frowned.

"I'm upset with you, Paul," said Santa. "You had a job to do. It was important. But you didn't do it."

Paul wanted to close his eyes again, but he didn't. "I'm sorry," he said.

"I know you are," Santa replied. "But you made a bad choice. You had a responsibility, and you

43

didn't take care of it. You almost burned down the forest."

Paul wanted to reply. He wanted to think of an excuse. He wanted to tell Santa that the forest fire wasn't his fault. But Paul knew that would be a lie.

The boy swallowed the lump in his throat. He squeezed the tears back into his eyes. "How can I make it better?" he asked.

"You can't fix this, Paul," said Santa. "The trees that burned are gone for good. But you can learn from it. From now on, be more responsible. Do the things you're supposed to do."

Paul nodded. "I will. I promise."

Santa smiled and patted Paul's arm. "Good. Now, let's get to work."

Emily joined their talk. "Do you have a plan?"

Santa replied, "We can't shrink that monster. So we need to fight it with something big. It's time

to find an old friend of mine. He lives nearby. His
name is Paul Bunyan."

9
Large Responsibility

"Paul Bunyan is real?" the children yelled.

Santa grinned. "Yes, but not how you think. Not any more. He's no taller than I am."

"I thought he was a giant," said Emily.

"Oh, he was," Santa replied. "But it's hard to be that tall. There was never a house to live in. There was never enough food to eat. And there was never anyone to play with."

Paul shrugged. "I guess that would be hard. How did he get small?"

"One Christmas, he asked if I could shrink him," said Santa. "I had an invention that could."

Paul's eyes opened wide. "The Shrink Wrapper!"

"That's right," said Santa. "Paul Bunyan is the only person I've ever shrunk. And I shrank his ox, Babe. Now, I need to make Paul Bunyan big again. He's our only chance to defeat the giant minotaur."

Paul remembered Santa's invention called the Growth Squirt. The Shrink Wrapper shrank gifts that Santa delivered at Christmas. The Growth Squirt returned them to normal size. It would probably do the same to Paul Bunyan.

Emily must have been thinking that, too. She said, "The Shrink Wrapper is broken. You can grow him. But you can't shrink him again."

Santa sighed. "Sadly, that's true."

"I'll talk to Paul Bunyan," said Paul. "I will get him to help us."

"Are you sure?" Santa asked. "This is very important, Paul."

"Yes," Paul replied. "I can be responsible. I will get it done."

Santa thought for a moment, then nodded. "I believe in you. We'll send you to Paul Bunyan." He looked at Emily. "I'll need your help, too."

"What can I do?" she asked.

"We have to keep the minotaur busy. So it won't do any more damage."

* * * * *

Santa Claus was right. Paul Bunyan lived nearby. Paul hiked to his cabin in less than an hour. The place wasn't much bigger than a garage. The cabin was made from chopped down trees—except for the chimney. That was made out of rocks.

Paul jogged to the front door, but he didn't have to knock. The door swung open.

The man who answered was about as tall as Santa. He had a lot more muscles, though. And his beard was black, not white. He wore jeans and a red flannel shirt.

"I know why you're here," Paul Bunyan snapped. "And I'm not going to help you!"

10
Paul Meets Paul

"Why won't you help us?" Paul asked.

Paul Bunyan answered, "I made that minotaur. It protects the Boundary Waters."

Paul's mouth opened wide, and so did his eyes. For a second, he could not think of any words.

At last, he asked, "How did you make it?"

Paul Bunyan grinned. "Oh, it was easy. I only needed two of Santa's inventions."

Paul thought about this. The minotaur looked like a man. But it had the head of a blue ox. Paul Bunyan must have used the Power Switch. He mixed a person with his pet, Babe the Blue Ox. Then he made the monster into a giant. For that, he must have used an extra bottle of Growth Squirt.

"I don't understand," said Paul. "How did you get Santa's inventions? Did you steal them?"

"No," Paul Bunyan answered. "Someone mailed them to me."

"Who?" asked Paul.

"I don't know, and I don't care. The minotaur is doing good work." Paul Bunyan didn't say another word. He slammed his cabin door shut.

* * * * *

Santa and Emily spotted the minotaur. It scooped up a mom, a dad, and three kids. It held them in its huge hands. Then it tossed them into a large lake. They landed with a *splash*.

"Help us!" the family cried.

The Super Spies paddled their Can News toward the victims.

"Are you okay?" yelled Santa.

"Yes, but save us!" replied the dad.

"What happened?" asked Emily. "Why did the minotaur throw you?"

"I don't know," said the mom. "We started a campfire. Then that monster came."

Santa looked at Emily. "Oh, dear," he said. "The minotaur thinks all fires are bad!"

The Super Spies pulled the family into their Can News. Then they paddled to safety.

* * * * *

Paul pounded on the door. He shouted, over and over, "The minotaur does not protect the forest!"

Paul Bunyan swung open the door. "It scares away bad campers," he snapped. "And it put out a forest fire that you started!"

Paul's cheeks grew warm. He looked at the ground and sighed. Then he lifted his head again. "That's true," he said. "But the minotaur is a giant monster. It tramples trees when it walks. It almost squished Santa. It could hurt somebody—or worse."

Now Paul Bunyan looked down and sighed. "I guess you're right," he said. "The minotaur has to be stopped. Turn me back into a giant."

11
Monster Battle

"Santa gave me his Growth Squirt," said Paul. "You can use it to get big. But first, I have bad news. The Shrink Wrapper is broken. You'll grow into a giant. But you can't turn small again."

Paul Bunyan flinched at the news. He pressed his hands over his eyes. Then he rubbed his fingers in his hair. He looked at Paul. "I can't do it," he said. "I won't stay a giant."

"But you have to," replied Paul. "You made that minotaur. So it's your responsibility to take care of it."

Paul Bunyan did not answer. He stared into the woods. He looked like he was thinking.

The Super Spy continued. "Sometimes, we know what we should do. But it's hard. We want to quit or give up. When we do the hard things, that makes us special. It makes us great. We work at them, and we do them—because it's right."

Paul Bunyan clapped his hands together. "All right, let's go and get that minotaur!"

* * * * *

Emily ran as fast as she could. She had been running for several minutes. The minotaur chased after her. This was the only way to keep it busy.

"Paul better hurry," she said. "I'm getting tired."

Boom!

The minotaur stopped running.

Boom!

It turned toward the new noise.

Boom!

The minotaur looked ready to fight. It stepped toward the sound.

Two large hands grabbed the monster's horns. "Babe," said Paul Bunyan. "It's time to end this. It's time to go home."

The minotaur glared at the giant man. It didn't seem to know him. It growled, and it shook. Paul Bunyan did not let go.

Roar!

The minotaur grabbed Paul Bunyan's waist. It lifted him and threw him like a toy doll.

Paul Bunyan landed hard. But he jumped back up. He charged the minotaur. This time, the beast smashed his stomach with its fist.

The giant man fell again. And again he stood. The minotaur pushed him with all of its might. Paul Bunyan flew backward.

The minotaur grabbed him again. It spun him around and around. When it let go, Paul Bunyan flew through the air. He landed in the lake with a great big *splash!*

"What are we going to do?" cried Emily. "The minotaur is too strong for Paul Bunyan!"

12
A Big Idea

Paul dashed to his friend Emily. He panted, trying to breathe. He had run all the way from Paul Bunyan's cabin.

"I . . . have an . . . idea," he gasped.

Santa raced to the children. "What is it, Paul? We need to act fast."

"I still have . . . some Growth . . . Squirt," the boy stammered.

Santa shook his head. "It won't work on us. I can't grow people unless they were big before."

"Not us," said Paul. "Our . . . gadget belts."

Santa lifted his head and smiled. "Ho! Ho! Ho! That might work!"

Paul, Emily, and Santa moved quickly. They put all of their gadgets into one belt. Paul gave Santa the Growth Squirt. Then the children backed away.

"I hope this works," said the jolly old man. He sprayed the gadget belt from one side to the other.

Nothing happened.

My plan didn't work, Paul thought.

The belt started to shake. It began to bounce. Then it grew. And grew. And grew.

"Yes!" Paul shouted. He jumped into the air.

Just then, rain began to fall. But the sky was blue. Paul looked up, and he grinned. He saw that it wasn't rain at all. Paul Bunyan stood next to him. He was dripping water from the lake.

The Super Spy pointed at the giant belt. "Put that on. Then pick me up. I'll tell you how to beat the minotaur."

* * * * *

Paul Bunyan rumbled toward the monster. His friend Paul sat on his shoulder. The minotaur saw the giant coming. It jumped out of the way—and it landed in the arms of the real Paul Bunyan.

The young Super Spy laughed. "It worked. That other Paul Bunyan wasn't real. It was a trick, made by our You-You gadget."

The minotaur struggled and squirmed. Paul Bunyan would not let go. The giant carried the monster to the lake. Then he threw it in.

"Now you're all wet!" Paul Bunyan belted.

The minotaur rose to its feet. It shook itself off, splashing water everywhere. The beast glared at Paul Bunyan. Its eyes looked like they were on fire.

"Now what?" Paul Bunyan asked Paul.

The boy answered, "Grab your giant Trouble Bubble bubble gum. Put it in your mouth, and chew it up."

Paul Bunyan did as he was told. He chomped on it quickly. The minotaur stomped out of the lake.

"Blow the biggest bubble that's ever been blown!" young Paul said.

The minotaur charged, and Paul Bunyan started to blow. The bubble was bigger than a house. Then it was bigger than a building. Then it was bigger than a football stadium.

Ka-boom!

The Trouble Bubble burst. It sounded like a bomb went off. It looked like a bubble gum blizzard.

Slowly, the pink storm ended. Paul could make out the shape of the minotaur. It was covered in the sticky gum.

Fireworks exploded in the sky. Paul heard Emily and Santa cheering below. "Hooray! You did it!"

The boy smiled. *This is the perfect end to the Minnesota mission.*

That's what Paul was thinking when the minotaur used its horns. The monster ripped itself free. And it growled.

13
Teamwork

Paul Bunyan bent over and put his hand on the ground. "We need a new plan," he told Paul. "Talk to the others."

Paul slid down his arm like a slide. He turned around to ask, "What are you going to do?" But Paul Bunyan was already charging toward the minotaur.

The three Super Spies came together. Ervin and Comet landed next to them.

"We saw the fireworks' blast," said Ervin. "So we came very fast!"

"I'm glad you did," said Santa. "We must work together. It's the only way to stop the minotaur."

"I wish we could give our skills to Paul Bunyan," said Emily. "Then he could win."

Paul snapped his fingers. "That's it! We can use the Power Switch."

Santa nodded. "Yes, that might work. Ervin, fly to the North Pole. Bring back the Power Switch."

"The Power Switch isn't in the North Pole," said Paul. "It's at Paul Bunyan's cabin."

"What?" Santa exclaimed. "How—" He shook his head. "Never mind. Ervin, take Paul with you. Go and get that Power Switch."

* * * * *

Paul Bunyan was still battling the minotaur—and still losing—when Paul got back.

The boy held the Power Switch in his hands. It looked like a light switch. Except it had two long cords sticking out of it.

"There are only two cords," said Santa. "That means we can only add one of us to Paul Bunyan. Whom should we choose?"

"Comet," replied Paul.

"Yes," added Emily. "He's fast, and he can fly."

"Good idea," Santa agreed. He unhooked Comet from the sleigh. Then he clipped one of the cords to the reindeer. "Now, we must clip the other cord to Paul Bunyan."

Paul and Emily hopped onto Comet's back.

"We'll take care of it," the boy said.

Comet leaped off the ground and zoomed toward the giant.

"When we get close," said Emily, "I'll jump onto Paul Bunyan. I'll hook the cord to him and slide off."

Paul told her, "I'll turn on the Power Switch. That will give Comet's powers to Paul Bunyan."

"I hope there isn't a firefly hiding in Comet's fur," said Emily. "Or Paul Bunyan will get a nose that glows!"

Paul would have laughed. But the minotaur slammed Paul Bunyan to the ground. It probably hurt Paul Bunyan. But Emily was able to jump onto his arm. She clipped the cord to him.

Comet landed next to the giant, and Paul hopped off. He waited for Emily to move away from Paul Bunyan. Then he switched on the machine.

The Power Switch started to hum. Several sparks shot out of the gadget. And then it shut off.

Emily shouted, "Did it work?"

"I think so," Paul answered. "Look!" He pointed at Paul Bunyan.

The large man was not on the ground any more. He was floating in the air. And reindeer horns were poking out of his head.

14
Good Work

The minotaur tried to grab Paul Bunyan. But the giant man flew out of the way. He soared into the sky like a falcon. He looped in the air and came behind the minotaur. He wrapped his arms around its waist and rocketed into the sky.

He dropped the minotaur. It landed with a loud *thud*. Paul Bunyan dove toward it.

The monster stood, and the giants' horns clashed. The minotaur shook its head in anger. But its horns were tangled in Paul Bunyan's antlers. Paul Bunyan pushed against the minotaur. It pushed against him. Neither could move the other. They were equal in strength.

But Paul Bunyan was smarter. He blasted off the ground, going up, up, up. He took the minotaur with him. The monster's face didn't look angry now. It looked scared. Its horns slid off the antlers, and the beast fell downward. This time, it landed in the lake with a *splash!*

The minotaur slowly made its way to shore. It looked too tired—and too scared—to fight. It crawled out of the water and dropped into the sand.

Paul Bunyan landed next to the monster. It looked at him for a moment. Then it looked away. It was beaten. It seemed ready to take anything that Paul Bunyan would do to it.

Paul Bunyan did not attack. He sat beside the creature. Then he petted the blue fur on its head.

* * * * *

"Good work, Super Spies," Santa said.

"What is going to happen with the minotaur?" Emily asked.

"Well, I've never un-switched powers before," Santa admitted. "My elves and I will work on a new invention. We should be able to reverse the Power Switch."

"That means Paul Bunyan will have Babe back," said Paul. "But does he have to stay a giant?"

"Ho! Ho! Ho!" Santa laughed. "I'll need a new Shrink Wrapper by Christmas. So Paul Bunyan can choose for himself."

Paul laughed too. "I'm glad. He's a good person. He should be happy."

"I agree," said Santa. "And speaking of good people, it's time to send you Super Spies home."

The sun began to set as the friends said goodbye to each other.

Santa patted Paul's arm. "Let me see your watch. I know right when to put you."

"*When?*" Paul asked. "Don't you mean *where?*" But then Paul got the joke. He remembered that his Super Spy watch could send him back in time.

Santa wound Paul's watch backward. When he finished, he waved. "I'll see you soon," he said.

Paul felt himself fade away. The Boundary Waters were gone. He was at home, talking to Matt.

He heard himself whisper, "You promised to help me take care of Rainy."

Matt smiled and nodded.

"Your job is to—" Paul stopped himself. "Your job is to hold a bag open. My job is to clean up the mess. I'll put it in the bag."

The two brothers worked together. Paul could tell that Matt felt proud of his work.

Paul felt proud, too. He had helped to stop the Minnesota Minotaur. And he had learned to take responsibility at home.

Epilogue

The children were both gone. Ervin was busy hooking Comet to the sleigh. Santa strolled over to Paul Bunyan.

"Thanks for your help," said the jolly old man.

"You're welcome," replied Paul Bunyan. "But if you didn't want a minotaur, why did you tell me to make one?"

Santa scratched his head. "Why do you think I told you?"

"A box was mailed to me from the North Pole," said Paul Bunyan. "The Growth Squirt and the

Power Switch were inside. There was also a book in the box. It told the myth about the hero Theseus and the minotaur."

"Was there anything else?" Santa asked.

"A note," Paul Bunyan answered. "It said, 'Protect the forest.' Didn't you send it to me?"

Santa shook his head. "No, I did not."

Paul Bunyan's eyes grew wide. "If you didn't, then who did?"

Santa shrugged his shoulders. "It's a mystery. And I plan to solve it."

"How can I help?" Paul Bunyan asked.

"By not making any more giant minotaurs," Santa answered with a wink.

The two friends laughed.

Get the Complete Collection of
Santa Claus: Super Spy Books

The Case of the Florida Freeze (#1)

The Case of the Delaware Dinosaur (#2)

The Case of the Colorado Cowboy (#3)

The Case of the Minnesota Minotaur (#4)

Super Spy State Challenge

Test your Super Spy knowledge with these questions about the state of Minnesota. If you get stumped, you can find the answers using the page numbers provided.

1. What is the capital of Minnesota? (Page 10)

2. What is Minnesota's state nickname? (Page 10)

3. Name three things that Minnesota is known for. (Page 10)

4. What place in the northern part of the state is perfect for fishing? (Page 11)

5. True or false? There are lots of buildings in the Boundary Waters. (Page 22)

6. True or false? Minnesota summers are hot, but winters are cold. (Page 10)

BONUS: As the legend goes, how were Minnesota's lakes made? (Page 12)

Did you answer them all?
Check your answers on the next page.

State Challenge Answers

1. Saint Paul

2. The Land of 10,000 Lakes

3. The Boundary Waters, the Mall of America, fishing, camping

4. The Boundary Waters

5. False. There are lots of trees, lakes, and islands. But there are not many buildings.

6. True

BONUS: The lakes were said to be made from Paul Bunyan's and Babe's footprints.

Did you enjoy this book?

If so, please consider reviewing it
at your favorite online store(s)
with your family or your class.

About the Author

Ryan Jacobson is the author of more than 40 books. He prides himself on telling high-interest stories for children of all ages.

Ryan's favorite part of being an author is getting to speak at schools. He loves to share his knowledge of and passion for storytelling.

Ryan lives in rural Minnesota with his wife and two children. For more information, visit his website at AuthorRyanJacobson.com.